I Love Vacations

by Anna Walker

For Klarissa, Georgia, and Kat

SIMON & SCHUSTER BOOKS FOR YOUNG READERS
An imprint of Simon & Schuster Children's Publishing Division
1230 Avenue of the Americas, New York, New York 10020
Text and illustrations copyright © 2008 by Anna Walker
First published by Scholastic Australia Pty Limited in 2008 as *I Love Holidays*
This edition published under license from Scholastic Australia Pty Limited
First U.S. edition 2011

SIMON & SCHUSTER BOOKS FOR YOUNG READERS
is a trademark of Simon & Schuster, Inc.
For information about special discounts for bulk purchases,
please contact Simon & Schuster Special Sales at 1-866-506-1949
or business@simonandschuster.com.
The Simon & Schuster Speakers Bureau can bring authors to your live event.
For more information or to book an event, contact the Simon & Schuster
Speakers Bureau at 1-866-248-3049
or visit our website at www.simonspeakers.com.
The text for this book is handwritten by Anna Walker.
The illustrations for this book are rendered in ink on watercolor paper.
Manufactured in Singapore / 0710 TIW
10 9 8 7 6 5 4 3 2 1
CIP data for this book is available from the Library of Congress.
ISBN 978-1-4169-8321-7

I Love Vacations

by Anna Walker

SIMON & SCHUSTER BOOKS FOR YOUNG READERS
New York • London • Toronto • Sydney

My name is Ollie.

I love vacations.

Fred is coming too.
Hooray!

I pick up shells

and splash

 by the sea.

I love the waves

and the waves love me!

I love to float,
watching the sky,

and see a turtle
swimming by.

I love sandy sandwiches

in the sun.

I love drippy ice cream,

I love the stars up in the sky
and the little owl hooting nearby.

too-whit-
toowooooo o

But what I love best
is to listen to the sea
singing softly
for Fred and me.